Rama's Journey

Narinder Dhami

Illustrated by
Carol Liddiment

An epic story from India

CONTENTS

OXFORD
UNIVERSITY PRESS

Dear Reader,

The story of the *Ramayana* is thousands of years old. The word 'Ramayana' means 'Rama's Journey'. There are lots of different retellings, this one is just *my* version.

When I was very young, my dad used to tell me the *Ramayana* story at bedtime. I loved hearing about Rama's adventures, but the ten-headed demon king, Ravana, gave me nightmares!

I hope you enjoy this story, the scary bits as well as the happy parts!

Narinder Dhami

Chapter 1

Once upon a time a king called Das lived in India. He ruled the green and beautiful kingdom of Kosala, and he lived there in a huge golden palace. The King had three wives and four sons, but his favourite son was his first-born, Rama.

• *Kosala:* (say) 'ko-sah-lah'. • *Rama:* (say) 'rah-muh'. **3**

Rama was the perfect prince. He was clever and handsome and brave, and he had a beautiful wife called Sita.

Now Das was very old by this time. He decided that he didn't want to be king any longer.

'It's time for someone else to rule this land,' the King thought. 'I know just the right person. My dear son, Rama!'

• *Sita:* (say) 'see-tuh'.

The people of Kosala were sad that their old king was leaving them, but they were delighted that Rama was taking his place. Everyone loved Prince Rama. They celebrated in the streets, singing and dancing and throwing flowers.

However, there was someone who wasn't happy to hear this news. One of the King's wives, Queen Kaik, was very angry indeed.

'Why should Rama rule this kingdom?' the Queen thought with a frown. 'My son, Bharata, would be a much better king than Rama!'

Suddenly the Queen had an idea that made her smile. Quickly she hurried off to find her husband.

The old King was walking in the palace gardens among the flowers and marble fountains.

'Sir, do you remember you once said that you would give me two wishes?' the Queen asked.

The King nodded. 'Of course I remember,' he replied. 'You saved my life when I was hurt in battle, and you looked after me until I was well again. I promised you then that I would grant you two wishes. You can have whatever you want.'

'Thank you,' the Queen said. 'First, I want you to make my son Bharata king in your place. Second, I want you to send Rama away to live in the wild forests for fourteen years.'

Chapter 2

The King was shocked.

'You don't mean that, my dear wife,' he begged. 'You can't ask me to send Rama away! You know how much I love him.'

'Oh, but I do mean it,' the Queen replied coldly. 'Bharata will be king, and Rama must leave this kingdom!'

The King spent a long time trying to get his wife to change her mind, but the Queen would not agree. So there was nothing the King could do. He called Rama to him and told him what the Queen had asked.

Rama was very upset. He didn't want to leave his home. However, he was a good son who always did as he was told.

'I'll go tomorrow, Father,' he said.

The King nodded. His eyes were full of tears.

Rama went to tell his wife Sita and his brother Laxman what had happened. Then he prepared to leave for the forests. He wanted to go alone, but his wife Sita wouldn't hear of it.

'I'm coming with you,' she said.

Rama frowned. 'Sita, the forests are dangerous,' he said. 'They're full of wild creatures like tigers and snakes. You're a princess, and you're used to living in a fine palace. I can't take you with me.'

'I'll be safe if I'm with you,' Sita said.

'I'm coming too,' said Laxman. He wasn't just Rama's brother, he was also his best friend.

Rama, Sita and Laxman changed their rich royal robes for simple old clothes. Then they left the palace. All the people gathered in the streets to watch them leave. Everyone was very sad to see them go.

King Das was so unhappy that he became ill. He took to his bed and none of the court doctors could cure him. A few days after Rama, Sita and Laxman left for the forests, the old King died of a broken heart.

'Now my son Bharata will be king instead of Rama!' the Queen thought happily.

Bharata had been away visiting his grandfather in a different land, so he didn't know what had happened. Now Bharata returned home to find his father dead and Rama, Sita and Laxman gone.

'What's this all about, Mother?' he asked
the Queen.

'My son, I asked your father to send Rama
away into the wild forests,' the Queen told
him. 'You are the new King of Kosala!'

Bharata couldn't believe it.

'What have you done, Mother?' he said.
'You know how much I love my brother
Rama. I'll look after the kingdom while he's
gone, but I won't take his place as king!'

Then Bharata took a pair of Rama's sandals and placed them on the glittering golden throne.

'This is to show everyone that my brother Rama is the true king,' Bharata said. 'And these sandals will stay here on the throne until Rama returns to his kingdom once more!'

Chapter 3

Rama, Sita and Laxman wandered through
the wild forests for many years. They ate fruit
and berries from the trees, drank water from
clear springs and slept on beds of grass.

At last they came to a beautiful river that
ran through a lush green valley.

'This is where we shall build our home,'
Rama decided.

So they built a hut out of bamboo, bark and twigs on the bank of the river. Sita made a garden around the hut and planted flowers, fruit and vegetables. The deer came to graze nearby, monkeys swung through the trees and the birds sang sweetly. Rama, Sita and Laxman were very happy, but they missed their family and friends back home.

They didn't know that someone was hiding in the trees watching them. It was Ravana, the King of the demons.

Ravana was a truly terrible demon. He was very tall and he had ten heads with twenty flashing dark eyes and ten arms. He was the best warrior in the world. No one had ever beaten him in a battle.

Ravana had heard many stories about Rama, Sita and Laxman, and so had come to see them for himself.

'Sita is very beautiful,' Ravana thought as he watched her in the garden. 'She should be my wife, not Rama's. I shall set a trap to kidnap her!'

Ravana sent a magical golden deer to graze on the grass near the hut. Sita's face lit up when she saw it.

'Rama, please catch that beautiful golden deer for me!' Sita begged him. 'I would love to have it for my pet!'

Rama nodded. Leaving Laxman to look after Sita, he ran quickly after the deer.

The deer led Rama away from the hut into the deepest, darkest part of the forest. Rama was just about to catch it when the deer called out in a loud voice, 'Oh, help me!'

Rama froze with shock. The deer's voice sounded exactly the same as his own!

'This is a trap!' Rama thought. 'I must get home as fast as I can.'

Back at the hut, Laxman and Sita had also heard the deer call out, in Rama's voice.

'Rama is in trouble!' Sita said. 'You must help him, Laxman.'

Laxman grabbed his bow and arrow and ran off into the forest. When he was gone, Ravana jumped out from his hiding place in the trees and ran over to Sita.

'Who are you?' Sita cried. She had never felt so frightened in her life.

'I am Ravana, King of the demons!' Ravana replied. He had an evil grin on all of his ten faces. 'I'm taking you to my kingdom of Lanka where you shall be my wife!'

Chapter 4

'No!' Sita shouted. 'I am Rama's wife, not yours!'

She tried to run away, but Ravana was too quick and strong for her. He grabbed Sita and dragged her away from the hut. Ravana's chariot and horses were hidden among the trees. The demon threw Sita into the golden chariot, jumped in after her and cracked his whip.

The horses rose up into the sky and galloped quickly through the clouds. Soon they were crossing the sea to the demon kingdom of Lanka.

Meanwhile, Rama met Laxman as he was
rushing through the forest.

'Brother, that deer was a trap!' Rama
panted. 'Where is Sita?'

Rama and Laxman dashed back to the hut.
To their dismay, Sita was gone.

'How will we ever find her?' Rama asked.

'I can help you!' called a voice high above them.

Rama and Laxman looked up. A golden eagle was sitting in the treetops.

'I saw the evil demon king, Ravana, kidnap your wife,' the eagle told Rama. 'He carried her away in his chariot to the island of Lanka.'

Rama was very angry.

'I will find Sita and bring her home,' he said, 'I shall make that demon pay for stealing my wife!'

'Let's go and look for Sita right away,' Laxman said.

The two brothers set off through the forests. They walked for many days, but Lanka was hundreds of miles away across the sea and Rama and Laxman did not really know the best way to get there.

After a while the brothers came to a clear, shining lake where they stopped to drink. Suddenly a monkey swung down from one of the trees.

'Hello!' he called. 'My name is Hanuman, and this is the kingdom of the monkeys. Who are you, my friends?'

'I am Rama, and this is my brother Laxman,' Rama replied. 'We're looking for the demon king, Ravana. He has kidnapped my wife and taken her across the sea to Lanka.'

'I'll be glad to help you!' Hanuman said. 'I'll take you to meet my monkey army.'

Then Hanuman began to grow. He grew bigger and bigger while Rama and Laxman watched in amazement. Soon Hanuman's head was in the clouds and he was no longer a little monkey. He was as tall as a mountain!

• *Hanuman:* (say) 'hun-oo-man'.

Chapter 5

Rama and Laxman stared up at Hanuman as
he towered over them.

'You must be a very special monkey!' Rama
said with a smile.

Hanuman nodded. 'I have magical powers,'
he said. 'I can change my shape and I can fly!'
He bent down low and shrank a little. 'Now
climb up onto my shoulders.'

Rama and Laxman did as Hanuman said.
Then Hanuman rose into the air and flew
quickly to the caves where he lived.

All the other monkeys gathered round
to hear the story of how Ravana had
kidnapped Sita.

'I shall go to Lanka and find out where Sita is,' said Hanuman.

'Take this, Hanuman,' Rama said. He handed the monkey his gold ring. 'Then Sita will know you're a friend. Tell her that I'll come and rescue her!'

Hanuman took a giant leap and soared up into the sky. Then he flew swiftly across India towards the island of Lanka. Because Hanuman was so big, he could fly very fast. Soon he looked down and saw the white-tipped waves of the sea below him. A few moments later he was flying over the island of Lanka.

'I wonder where Sita is?' Hanuman thought. As he flew down to land, he shrank back to his small size. 'I shall look for her in Ravana's palace.'

Ravana's palace was right in the middle
of the city. It was night-time, and Hanuman
hid in the shadows so that the guards didn't
spot him. Quietly he slipped through the
golden gates into the palace gardens. There
Hanuman peeped around a tree and saw
Ravana. The monkey also saw a circle of one
hundred ugly demons. In the middle of the
demons sat a beautiful woman. Hanuman
could see that she looked very sad.

'You're such a foolish girl, Sita!' Ravana shouted angrily. 'I can give you clothes and jewels, and more riches than you can ever dream of! What can that husband of yours give you? A hut in a forest!'

'I don't care,' Sita replied. 'I will never marry you!'

'Then you will be my prisoner for ever!' Ravana roared. 'You'll never escape while my demons guard you!'

'Rama will come and rescue me,' Sita said. 'I know he will!'

Hanuman felt the ground shake as Ravana stomped angrily away. The monkey waited until all the demons guarding Sita had fallen asleep. Then he slipped out and hurried over to her.

'I come from Rama,' Hanuman whispered. 'He said to give you this.'

Hanuman gave Sita the ring, and she smiled.

'I knew he'd find me!' she said.

'Rama will come to rescue you and rid Lanka of Ravana for ever!' Hanuman told her. But right at that moment the ugliest demon woke up.

'Quick, grab that monkey!' the demon shouted.

Chapter 6

'Oh, be careful!' Sita called as Hanuman began to fight with the demons.

Hanuman knew he could escape from the demons, but he wanted to have some fun with them first.

So he made himself very big, and the demons screamed in terror. Then Hanuman made himself very tiny. Laughing, he ran off through the garden and hid among the flowers.

'Where is that monkey?' the demons yelled as they rushed here and there. 'Ravana will be very angry if we don't catch him!'

Hanuman had a secret plan. He wanted to meet Ravana and find out how big the demon king's army was. So at last he changed to their size and let the demons catch him. They tied him up tightly with rope and dragged him away.

Hanuman pretended to be very frightened
when the demons took him to their king.
Ravana was sitting on his wonderful golden
throne. Slowly he turned all of his ten heads
to glare at Hanuman.

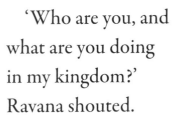

'Who are you, and what are you doing in my kingdom?' Ravana shouted.

'I am Hanuman,' Hanuman replied, 'and I'm here to tell you that Rama is coming to rescue Sita with an army of monkeys!'

Ravana's ten faces turned red with anger.

'Set fire to the monkey's tail!' he roared.

The demon guards brought flaming torches and tried to set fire to Hanuman's tail. Hanuman smiled and kept making his tail grow longer and longer so that the demons couldn't grab the end of it.

At last Hanuman let them catch his tail
and set fire to it. He gave a mighty roar that
shook the palace roof. Then Hanuman made
himself big and burst the ropes that tied him.

'I'll be back with Rama and my army!'
Hanuman told Ravana.

Hanuman jumped out of the window and
flew away over the city. As he went, he set fire
to the buildings with the tip of his burning
tail. The city blazed behind him as Hanuman
flew towards the sea.

'Oh, that's better!' Hanuman sighed as
he dipped his tail in the water and put the
fire out.

Then he headed home to India to prepare
for the battle with Ravana and his demons.

Chapter 7

Rama, Laxman and all the monkeys were waiting for Hanuman.

'I have seen Sita!' Hanuman told them. 'She is well, but she's guarded by one hundred ugly demons. Ravana will never let her go.'

'Then we shall march to Lanka and defeat Ravana!' Rama said.

Hanuman and all the monkeys cheered.

The next day Rama, Laxman, Hanuman and the huge army of monkeys set out on their long journey. They marched for many days until at last they reached the wide blue sea. They could just see the island of Lanka far away in the distance.

'We must build a bridge to cross the sea to Lanka,' said Rama.

Some of the monkeys began collecting
large rocks and others cut down tall trees.
They rolled them onto the shore and then
pushed them all into the water. Then they
added smaller rocks and more trees on top.
It took Rama, Laxman, Hanuman and the
monkey army many weeks to make a bridge
long enough to reach Lanka. But at last it
was finished.

'You've done well, my friends!' Rama called
when the last rock was put in place. 'Now let
us cross the sea to Lanka!'

The monkey army marched across the bridge with Rama, Laxman and Hanuman at the front.

But when they reached the other side, Ravana was waiting for them with his demon army.

Chapter 8

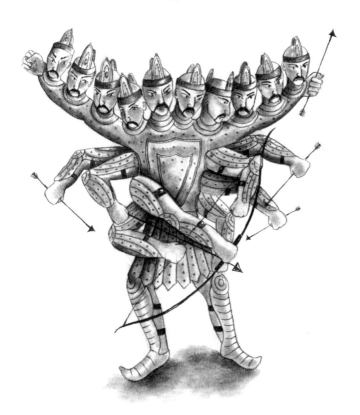

Ravana wore a suit of shining golden armour.
He held a bow in one of his ten hands and
had many arrows.

'You have dared to bring your army to my
kingdom, Rama!' Ravana roared furiously.
'I shall make you pay with your life!'

Ravana fired his arrows at the monkey army, and the battle began. The demons rushed forward and began fighting the monkeys. They fought for days and many demons and monkeys were hurt, but neither side would give in.

'Out of my way!' Ravana shouted as he raced across the battlefield. 'I shall kill Rama and put an end to his army once and for all!'

Hanuman and Laxman were standing close to Rama. They saw Ravana rushing towards them, and they shot arrows at him. The arrows sliced off some of Ravana's heads, but new ones always grew back in their place.

Soon Rama and Ravana stood face to face.

'You'll be sorry you kidnapped my wife, Ravana!' Rama shouted.

'Be quiet, you fool!' Ravana sneered. 'You'll never defeat me!'

Rama and Ravana began to fight as the monkeys and demons watched. They battled for many hours, but Ravana could not get the better of Rama. Nor could Rama's arrows pierce the King's shining armour.

Then Rama remembered a special, golden arrow that had been given to him by the gods. Quickly he drew back his bow and sent the fiery arrow shooting through the air towards Ravana. The magic arrow pierced the demon's armour and went through his heart.

Ravana roared loudly and fell down dead. Hanuman, Laxman and the monkey army shouted for joy.

Quickly Hanuman ran to fetch Sita from the palace and brought her to Rama.

'My dear husband!' Sita said with tears in her eyes. 'I knew you would come and rescue me!'

Rama, Laxman and Sita thanked Hanuman and his monkey army for being good and brave friends. Then they went back across the bridge and set off for Kosala. The fourteen years were now over, and Rama could become king.

The people of Kosala were waiting for
them. They clapped and cheered, and lamps
were lit in every window to welcome Rama,
Sita and Laxman home. Even the Queen was
sorry for what she had done, and was glad to
see them.

Rama's brother, Bharata, was filled with joy.
He took Rama's sandals off the throne and
gave them back to him.

'Now the real king is home!' Bharata
said happily.

Rama was crowned King of Kosala. He
was a good and wise king, and he ruled the
land for many years with his wife Sita and
his faithful brothers, Laxman and Bharata,
at his side.